D1472312

THE BOY AND THE BOY KING

by GEORGE H. LEWIS and A.D. LUBOW

with illustrations by GEORGE H. LEWIS

First published in 2020 by
The American University in Cairo Press
113 Sharia Kasr el Aini, Cairo, Egypt
One Rockefeller Plaza, New York, NY 10020
www.aucpress.com

Dar el Kutub No. 26513/19
ISBN 978 977 416 997 7

Dar el Kutub Cataloging-in-Publication Data

Lewis, George H.
  The Boy and the Boy King / George H. Lewis, A.D. Lubow.—Cairo: The American University in Cairo Press, 2020.
    p.   cm.
  ISBN 978 977 416 997 7
  1. Children's literature. English
  2. Children's stories, English
        808.0683

1 2 3 4 5   24 23 22 21 20

Printed in China

"May we all grow up to be children."
—Bun-Bun

For Ellie and Charlotte who know more than any adult could ever imagine.
—George H. Lewis and A.D. Lubow

1

One day not so long ago a package arrived in the mail, all the way from England. A little boy named Arthur opened it with great anticipation.

Inside was a pair of stuffed rabbits: Arthur immediately named them Bun-Bun and Bunabooboo. All Bunabooboo wanted to do was sleep.

But straight out of the box Bun-Bun came alive. He was something of a character: pompous and postulating, full of compassion for others, but also a little full of himself. To this day, if you call him an "imaginary" friend, you'll never hear the end of it:

"Imaginary? I mean really! The cheek of it! I'm as real as can be! Yes, I'm just a stuffed animal. And certainly, I admit it, I can be a little stuffy. But actually, I am a wonderfully bright, terribly English, jolly clever bunny!"

Arthur and Bun-Bun became best friends.

Arthur was just an ordinary boy in New York City, a place where it is difficult to remain a boy for long. All of his classmates were eager to grow up fast, as though childhood were a race to be won.

Arthur, by contrast, was in no hurry. He was content to wile away his afternoons with his toys, his book on magic tricks, and his Bun-Bun.

"You take your time, Arthur," Bun-Bun said. "There's no rush, nobody's going anywhere. It's the journey that matters."

Bun-Bun wasn't in a hurry—not by any stretch of the imagination. He'd often take time to summer at Bunnykenport with the rich and famous of the imaginary friend set. He read a lot. Time Travel & Leisure was his favorite magazine.

Arthur's mother was an archaeologist who studied Egypt.

"Yes, Arthur, I'm an Egyptologist. And I'm your mummy," she joked, "but I like the way you call me Mum-Mum."

At bedtime, Mum-Mum told Arthur stories of pyramids, tombs, and golden scarabs. The stories he loved best were all about Tutankhamun, the boy king. Tut was only nine-years-old when he became the ruler of a whole kingdom. Arthur was of a similar age and, in his mind, commanded a kingdom of his own.

When Arthur dreamed, he dreamed he was a boy king—so much so that when he looked into the mirror he sometimes saw the reflection of a king.

Bun-Bun encouraged this type of behavior. "Imagination rules, remember my boy! The magic of today is the science of tomorrow."

When Arthur was younger, he took Bun-Bun with him everywhere and no one said a thing. Then, on the first day of the new school year, things changed. Someone pointed. There were words whispered in corners and sharp little laughs. At recess, a girl wagged her finger at Arthur and when he was close, she put her mouth right up to his ear. "We're too old for stuffed animals," she said coldly. And then the boys started to tease. Ultimately Arthur's teacher, Ms. Severe, threatened to take Bun-Bun away. Arthur wouldn't let her. He began hiding Bun-Bun.

Yes, it's true: imaginary friends do spend a lot of time hidden away in book bags, which explains why Bun-Bun became so very well read.

Still, Ms. Severe would ask Arthur: "Why can't you go anywhere without this silly Bon-Bon of yours?"

The mispronunciation of his name absolutely infuriated Bun-Bun, who would complain, "I say, what kind of a teacher doesn't know the difference between a proper name and a pretentious piece of chocolate?"

Then one day in the park, Ms. Severe caught Arthur speaking to Bun-Bun behind a tree. Oops! That was the last straw.

8

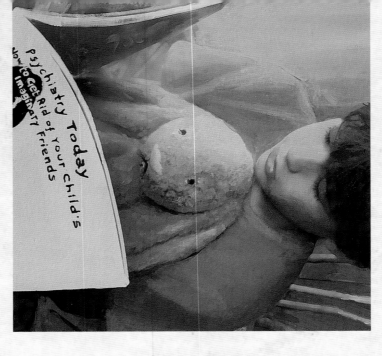

"You need to speak to the principal and the school psychologist!" Ms. Severe scolded.

"I don't NEED a psychologist," Arthur answered. "I have Bun-Bun!"

Bun-Bun and Arthur both chuckled.

"What you need is to get rid of that toy, that imaginary friend," said the humorless Ms. Severe.

"Bun-Bun is my REAL friend," Arthur said fiercely, but Ms. Severe only pursed her lips more, handing over a frightful pamphlet to prove her point.

Bun-Bun's nose twitched with horror. "This is absolute piffle," he cried out into Arthur's ear. "When times get tough, imagination is a boy's best friend."

But as soon as Ms. Severe departed, her co-teacher, Miss Gutkind, one of Arthur's favorites, appeared right on the scene. Noticing Arthur all alone and rather sad, she walked straight over to him and pulled a beautiful leather-bound book from her bag, handing it to him: *The Book of Magical Friends*.

"Read this tonight," she said. "I hope you'll find it helpful. I did when I was your age, and I still do."

Bun-Bun had a strange, almost conspiratorial look about him, as if Miss Gutkind was doing his bidding.

That night, Arthur and Bun-Bun began reading the book that Miss Gutkind had given them, their imaginations running wild. "Isn't it funny," Arthur remarked, "the characters almost look like us?"

After lights-out, Arthur and Bun-Bun shed their covers and their cares, walked to the bay window, opened the curtains, and looked down upon the millions of twinkling lights in the city and then toward the vast canopy above. "They say our future is in our stars," Bun-Bun observed, "but, remember my lad, our past is in our stars, too. Life is stardust spiraling over time, stardust that has been swirling around on Earth for so long that it has forgotten from where it came. Did you ever wonder about that, Arthur?"

"Earth to Bun-Bun, come in, Bun-Bun. Look at Ms. Severe's pamphlet! We're in big trouble, Bun-Bun. What will we do?" pleaded Arthur.

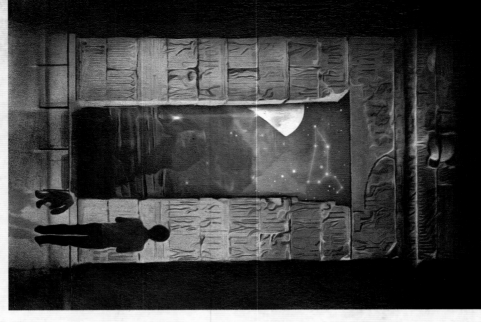

That weekend Arthur insisted on taking his mother to one of his favorite places in the city: the Temple of Dendur in the Metropolitan Museum.

The Temple was an enormous stone building, tattooed with hieroglyphics, built thousands of years ago in Egypt.

Looking at this ancient building with its timeless inscriptions, Arthur thought to himself: "I wonder why Bun-Bun wanted to come here?"

As if reading his mind, Bun-Bun said, "I'll explain, but I need more than a moment. Tell Mum-Mum you're parched."

With that, Mum-Mum offered to fill Arthur's water bottle, cautioning: "And you just stay right where you are! I'll be back . . . in no time."

Arthur and Bun-Bun were now alone in a room that was empty and almost silent.

"Do you see it?" Bun-Bun said, pointing, as he peered into the doorway of the tomb filled with ancient stellar alignments.

There was a strange light coming from inside the temple.

Arthur looked around to make sure no one was watching, then stepped over a security rope that blocked the passage through the doorway. There within, all dressed in gold and black and bathed in light, appeared a boy. He stood silently calling them in before he vanished into the glow.

Arthur and Bun-Bun followed him into the light. Beneath them, through a portal in time and space, Arthur could see a vast landscape emerging.

"We appear to be riding a moonbeam," Bun-Bun said calmly, as if he had done this many times before. "There are deep dark holes in the universe where the ancient and the new are one. This is such a place," said Bun-Bun.

2

In his dream, Arthur had an unquenchable thirst. When he awoke, he knew why. This was more than a dream. He found himself in the driest place on Earth. There was sand as far as the eye could see. Arthur shook Bun-Bun awake in disbelief.

There were no buildings, no people, no trees, and no water in sight. Perched upon a tiny rock within a sea of dunes a sudden wave of hopelessness washed over Arthur, indeed crashed over him like a breaking wave. Real tears welled up in the corner of Arthur's eyes. Oh, how he wished he had his water bottle now. Oh, how he wished for Mum-Mum.

"Now, now," Bun-Bun said. "The soul dreams dreams within a sea of dunes. But your spirit has to keep walking. Let's look for the source of energy and creation. Let's go toward the sun. Ra! Let's find our own star."

They would soon come upon a caravan of camels trudging in a snaky line toward a pyramid that pointed to a shooting star flashing for a moment as if the heavens had been made by humans and the pyramids had been built by an intelligence from far beyond.

Nighttime is the daytime of the desert. Near a cluster of pyramids, our travelers stumbled across a camp of nomads who seemed to be awakening as the sun went down.

By a campfire, under a shower of shooting stars and ancient stories, the strangeness of the nomads' language melted away and Arthur was delighted to discover he could understand every word. Amid the mingling aromas of frankincense, juniper, rose, and myrrh, the nomads described mysterious beauties near and far.

The waters are mighty at flood time,
O night, my love forever.
Escape from the presence of hardship,
The muse and the madness of prophecy,
The mystic rites of love.

Arthur had no idea whatsoever what any of this meant, and yet his entire body shivered with its ancient wisdom.

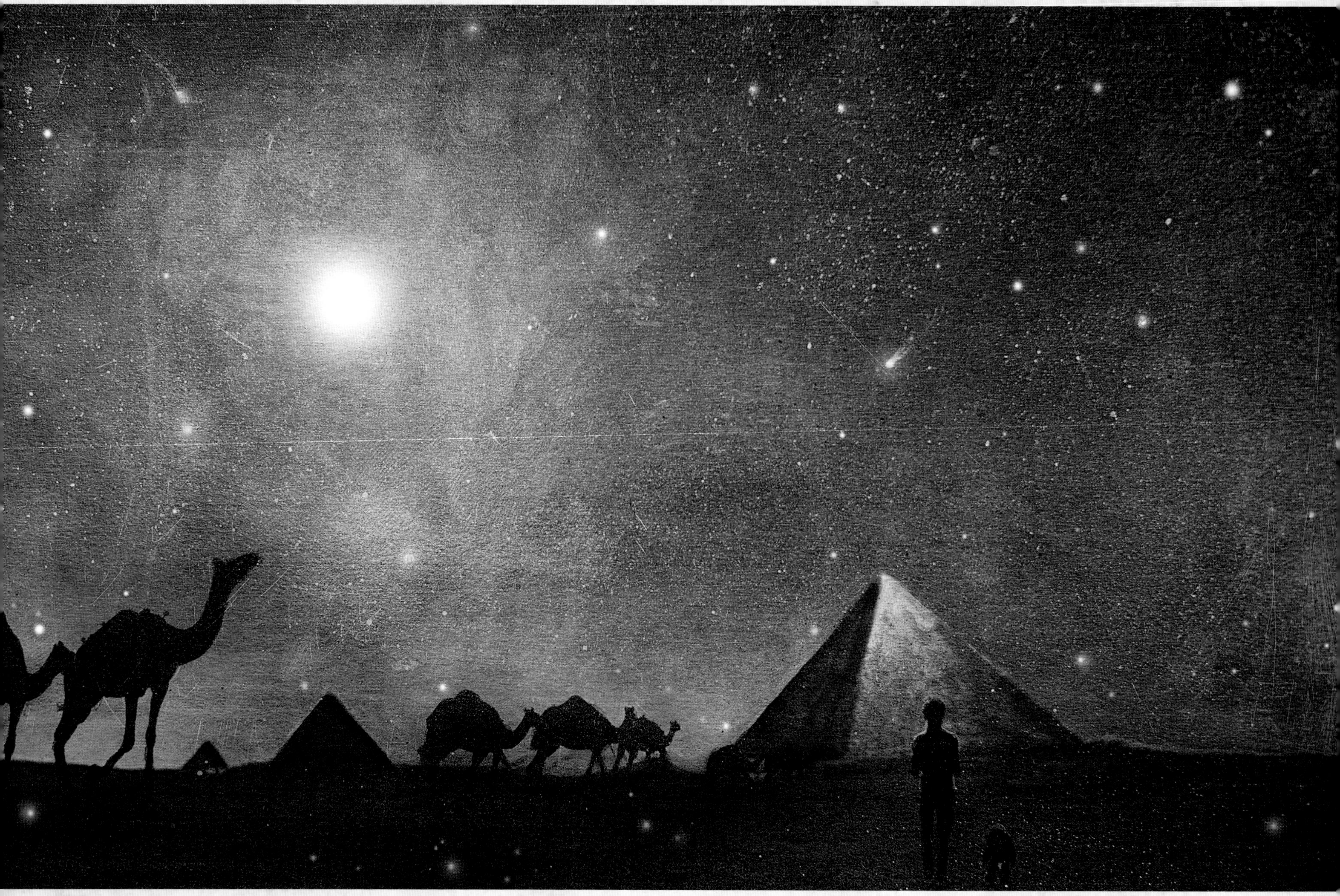

Guided by the light of the heavens, Arthur grew brave enough to ask, "Where are you going?"

"To Thebes, for an audience with the king," answered the tribal elder. "We seek funds to build a riverside dock in our village, so that the fishermen may prosper."

"Which king?" Arthur asked.

"Tutankhamun, of course, the boy king." said the tribal leader.

After a few days' journey, the caravan came to a walled city teeming with life. The air smelled of leather and mint and camel dung and straw.

They passed through the gate and made their way along a wide boulevard, finally reaching the great palace. There, they saw a long line of petitioners awaiting an audience with the king. In the distance, seated upon a dais, sat His Majesty. They joined the queue.

Hours passed. Finally fed up, Bun-Bun jumped ahead of everyone and rushed to the front. Arthur instinctively followed.

"Hold on, who's that bunny?" said the boy king as he saw this rabbit quickening toward him.

"That's Bun-Bun, Your Majesty," Arthur said spontaneously. "He's not accustomed to waiting in line."

"Guards, seize them! And make them sit on the bench by the pool," Tut said sternly. "I will deal with them momentarily; for now I must continue with official proceedings."

Arthur was shocked to realize that he had suddenly come face-to-face with Tutankhamun—the boy king himself. Even though Tut sat on his throne, formal and upright, his eyes told the truth that he was exhausted beyond his years, exhausted by the very act of kingship. On both sides of the young king hovered a pair of advisors with strange tunics, golden earrings, and shifty eyes. One of them handed Tut a cup to drink from, and Arthur noticed the boy king's resistance. Arthur instantly thought of Ms. Severe and her advisors and their weird pills and prescriptions.

"No, we don't need medicines," cried Arthur and Tut both at once and as one.

"Success!" thought Bun-Bun.

Soon the elder nomad, with whom Arthur had traveled, stepped to the front of the line, bowed deeply, and made his petition for a fishing pier to help the people of his village.

"Your Majesty must deny the request of these common liars," insisted the advisor on the right, still holding a tonic over Tut. "We need the riverfront for vital defenses."

"They're NOT liars," Arthur blurred. In a flash, the king's guards drew their swords against him.

A fellow boy's courage had set off a transformation in Tut. He suddenly seemed to awaken, eyes sparkling, causing the sad little king to announce in defiance:

"STOP! STOP."

And the guards stood down.

"Who is this strange boy in bizarre clothes who dares to speak?"

"I'm Arthur, sir; I am with Bun-Bun." Bun-Bun took a modest bow.

Tut intrigued and enlivened by this set of events, paused, thought, and addressed the court: "The river is a not a place of war, it's a place for granaries and fisheries; it's a place for peace. Let us build the dock so our children can learn to fish."

One of Tut's advisors began to splutter: "But, Your Majesty, you've never refused our counsel before!"

Tut looked at Arthur and said to his advisor, "It's true. Lots of pharaohs need help. But you're all trying too hard. What I need is a friend."

Arthur had felt the same thing many times before. Tut led them away.

"Oh how predictable" he retorted. Arthur then pulled *The Emperor* and finally Tut selected a card, gazed at it for a moment, and turned ashen white, saying:

"We just can't keep playing in the palace, I am worried that my advisors will see me doing this."

"Then we'll sneak out," Arthur replied.

Using a blanket as a disguise, Tut was soon un-recognizable.

Just then they heard footsteps from behind and guards yelling: "INTRUDERS!"

They made a sudden dash for it down a long stone corridor lined with statues of great pharaohs, through a courtyard, and out onto the streets.

Freedom!

The king's chambers were many times the size of Arthur's apartment in New York. There were gilded toys and rare fabrics studded with rubies. Bun-Bun and Arthur, standing beside an almost untouched sword collection, wondered what to make of all this paraphernalia.

Tut entered the room silently, "My father died before he could teach me the art of swordplay.

The truth is, I'm not allowed to play with any of these things."

"Such a waste," Bun-Bun muttered.

"It's all right," Tut said. "I never knew my father. But I want to know who you are. Are you from the northern kingdom or the southern kingdom?"

"I'm from the upper east side . . . kingdom," Arthur replied nervously.

"I've never heard of it," Tut said. "But it's difficult to keep track sometimes, my advisors have me twisted into such knots."

"Why do you listen to them?" Arthur asked.

Looking down, Tut was silent and sad. Bun-Bun reached into his pocket for his favorite deck of mag-ical cards that he carried for moments just like these.

"Are you going to keep staring? Or shall we see what the cards have to say?" insisted Bun-Bun.

"Let's play!"

"Play?" Tut laughed scornfully. "Kings aren't allowed to play!"

"But boys are," Arthur replied. "You're a boy king. So let's do it!"

And so the cards began to reveal their sacred mysteries. Bun-Bun shuffled the deck and pulled out *The Magician*.

"That was absolutely exhilarating!" the king exclaimed, his eyes shining. "Now let's play hide-and-seek in the market-place."

And when the boy and the boy king tired of that, they bought a handful of dates and sat on the banks of the river, spitting the pits out and laughing as Bun-Bun did handstands.

Oh, the fun a boy and a boy king can have, taking turns swinging over the banks of the Nile. From dream to reality and back again did Arthur swing.

Next, they sailed the boy king's favorite boat down the great river. The views were spectacular, but the boys gave most of their attention to a right royal stinky bug collection that they had dragged up to the poop deck. Boys (and boy kings) will be boys!

And by the time the sky began to twinkle and the sun prepared to set, Tutankhamun was no longer a boy king, but simply a boy.

Bun-Bun thought this the most marvelous thing he'd ever seen, for children when at play, engaging with their imaginations, have no need for strange pills or tonics. Bun-Bun could barely keep up as the boys shared their newfound freedom. Arthur and Tut came from different time zones, yet they waged friendship, not war.

When Tut went away to get his chariot, Arthur and Bun-Bun saw what seemed like a very familiar sight: a wild stallion galloping out of nowhere.

"Look, Bun-Bun, the Horse from *The Book of Magical Friends!*"

"Tally-ho!" bellowed Bun-Bun.

"It's us in the book, isn't it, Bun-Bun?" Arthur asked.

"Yes, sir, it's been us all along," said Bun-Bun.

Tut hitched two of his prized horses to his favorite chariot and gave the reins to Arthur and Bun-Bun, who gasped at the utter thrill of kicking up the sand and driving on their own. Bun-Bun yelled out at the top of his lungs: "The magic of childhood soars like a chariot in time and space!" He sang it out loud for no one but Arthur and the desert to hear. It was all beyond happiness.

"Sheer moonlit eudaimonia!" said Bun-Bun in his very bookish way.

It was only when Tut hitched the magical white horse to his chariot did it rise up from the ground and into the starry sky. "Houston, we have lift off!" exclaimed Arthur.

The day was a dream, the dream was a day.

Both Tut and Arthur were utterly astounded by the speed at which the chariot ascended.

"Wow, Tut" exclaimed Arthur as he glanced back down to Earth looking at the patterns that the pyramids made.

"Incredible" said Tut staring down. Then the boys, glancing up, saw a mirror image of the same pyramids, but this time in the stars above.

"As above, so below" said Bun-Bun, relishing the awe on the faces of the boys. "You see, those stars above belong to Orion and are in perfect alignment with the great pyramids. It was all very well planned."

They returned to Earth with a bit of a bump, landing next to the Great Sphinx.

Yes, this leonine creature (who had held a rather uncomfortable pose serving very bossy people for what must have seemed like an eternity) was in fact under a lot of pressure at work, controlling floods and harvests in good times and bad. This creature, part lion, part human—some say more woman, some say more man—had long suffered the challenges brought on by her multiple identities.

Bun-Bun jumped up onto the Sphinx's paw and began to whisper prophecy, foretelling the possibility of this future age, the Aquarian Age about to rise, a time of acceptance and peace. And it was so, that the Sphinx, feeling enchanted, strangely at ease, for the first time in millennia, did drop her head to her paws like a puppy dog and fall into a deep sleep.

"Tut, did you hear what I heard Bun-Bun say? Was he talking about a time of no war?" Arthur asked keenly.

The cosmos smiled as if it had a plan, as if imagination itself was one of the seven wonders of the world. It was then that the boy king had a premonition that peace would one day triumph over war.

The next morning Arthur and Tut woke up to the most unexpected of sights. The waves of the sea had crept up upon the desert dunes. Bun-Bun, staring out at the water, bathed in the morning light, was strangely repeating:

"The desert remembers. The desert remembers its life at the bottom of the sea. The silicon in the sand remembers and will one day rule. The desert shall become the pharaoh. This is the desert remembering, this is the desert imagining. This is the cosmos veiled in mathematics and music. This is our childhood lasting forever."

Tut, having no idea what Bun-Bun was talking about, simply said: "Don't you think I should return to my responsibilities at the palace?" Bun-Bun nodded "Press on . . ." in affirmation.

But Bun-Bun's incantations had stirred the imagination of Tut, and he began thinking deeply about his own destiny. A raven started circling in the sky above him as he hurried back, Arthur and Bun-Bun following close behind.

Back at the palace, Tut was greeted with surprise and relief. His courtiers fawned over him and whipped up a feast to celebrate his return.

Later, in the king's chamber, Arthur and Bun-Bun were alone with Tut. "Don't you want to play anymore?" Arthur asked.

"You can't know how much I want to play. How much I want to live happily . . . live happily ever after, as the stories go. But I must put my own desires aside, so come with me," Tut implored. Arthur and Bun-Bun followed him to the roof of the palace.

"Look into the distance, look in all directions," Tut pointed. "Here to the right is our great Nile, with its vast and verdant floodplains that nourish our people. You can see, there's a harmony to it. But on the left," he sighed, "all you see is fire,

disease, and destruction. It's a place where people are enslaved, unable to breathe, let alone evolve."

Arthur was terror-stricken because he'd never seen anything like this. Bun-Bun, on the other hand, was horrified because he'd seen it all before.

"Time after time," Bun-Bun said, "They don't learn: man against man; man against planet! But Tut, in every age there is a powerful winged stallion, the imagination that lifts us out, if we are ready. A person with a dream. Every child pure of heart must use every ounce of their imagination to send us soaring beyond the reach of the unevolved and corrupt. You understand now?"

"Yes, I believe I do," said Tut, as he looked out at the contrasting landscape and the choices ahead. "I must fight for my kingdom now for the sake of kingdoms to come. As a boy and as a king I must imagine . . . I simply must imagine something better. And speak it. Loudly."

Bun-Bun was utterly moved by the boy king's sudden growth and the divine wisdom that was emanating from within. Bun-Bun felt at long last that Tut was ready to hear what he had to say:

"Tut," advised Bun-Bun, "humanity is a species of high intellect but our baser instincts still need to evolve. We could stay with you and guide you spiritually to a peaceable outcome. There may still be time."

Though Bun-Bun had seen one future, a darker future, he also held a deep power of practical imagination that could shift and create a more evolved timeline and an alternative. If he could see a new path with Tut, he might make the world work out differently.

Tut didn't understand it fully, but was on board. Arthur, on the other hand, was growing homesick—and Tut could see that.

"Tut," said Arthur, "I'm not needed here. It's Bun-Bun who should stay behind. He will be your imagination and your friend. You can make history . . . together."

Bun-Bun, torn between his soul mates and a labyrinth of cosmic choices, swept his arm dramatically to the vaulting night sky and said: "We are all passengers on a swirling ball in space and somewhere within, I can be with you both . . . always. Deep into the distant galaxies is the pull of love that drives us here on Earth. You'll find me there, in the far-off stars where everything began and childhood never ends."

"That's all fine, Bun-Bun, but I'll miss you terribly."

Arthur's eyes were glassy but Bun-Bun stood stoically, arms crossed.

"Yes," said Tut. I know now that love and light, above all else, shall rule. You and Arthur taught me what matters: sailing and swinging and make-believe and fishing and card games and fast horses and chariots and even a stinky bug collection. I want to be a boy forever. And I want to show the world how wonder and imagination can work, when left alone to play. Bun-Bun, will you stay and help me? Will you be my imagination? Will you be my guide, but most of all, will you be my friend? Somehow, I believe it's my destiny to help the world by living as a boy, and thus a king, for all time."

Arthur, now pointing to the distant stars, agreed: "Yes, it's your turn, Tut, to change the world, if not now, someday."

Quietly crying, Arthur offered Tut his hand. Tut, ignoring all kingly protocol, pushed Arthur's arm aside and hugged him deeply and profoundly.

"How resplendent are our auras, full of so many inexplicable emotions," Bun-Bun commented, taking Arthur's hand. Arthur's courage was exemplary as Bun-Bun led him through the light of the Hall of Osiris to a doorway into certainly an uncertain future. A heroic journey, indeed.

Tut exclaimed: "What's happening, Bun-Bun?"

Bun-Bun calmly said: "It's just as I've described many times to Arthur: if time has no beginning or end, and if starlight can evolve into thought, why can't thought spiral back and ahead into light? Yes, the past as well as the future is in our stars."

"Well, here I go," said Arthur as he let go of Bun-Bun, walking slowly toward the portal.

"Arthur!" cried Bun-Bun. Arthur turned around.

Bun-Bun hopped into his arms and whispered, "I'll miss you, too, my boy."

Arthur, speechless, tears streaming down his cheeks, set Bun-Bun down on the ground.

"We'll meet in the stars," Arthur said, vanishing into another time and place.

3

Back at the Temple of Dendur, Arthur's mother suddenly returned. "Oh, there you are! I was looking all over for you. It seemed like you'd disappeared for ages."

Arthur only wanted to know one thing:

"Mum-Mum, are men still at war?"

Arthur's mother thought this a strange thing to ask, but said, "Yes, my darling," and she paused, "I'm afraid so."

Arthur found it hard to breathe for a moment.

"Mum-Mum, what happened to King Tut? Did he have a long reign and was he able to bring peace to his people? What do the books say?"

Mum-Mum replied, "Oh, Arthur, sadly no, he was murdered when only a boy. Most historians suspect he was betrayed by his ministers—all but one that is, a devoted friend who remained behind the scenes guiding him."

"Oh, Bun-Bun, oh, of course, Bun-Bun," grieved Arthur silently.

"I'd like to go home now."

They left the museum in silence and caught a cab on Fifth Avenue. It wasn't until they were back home, taking off their shoes, that Arthur's mother noticed:

"Oh no! Did we leave Bun-Bun in the museum? We should go back!"

"No, not in the museum, he's in Egy . . ." Arthur stopped himself suddenly. "It's okay."

"Are you really sure?" Mum-Mum wondered.

"It's okay," Arthur repeated. "Bun-Bun will be fine wherever he goes."

Mum-Mum smiled curiously. After a brief pause, though, Arthur couldn't help but continue: "I think Bun-Bun had some remarkable superpowers and he wanted to help King Tut restore his father's faith and vision for the kingdom. He wanted to create a civilization devoted to art and knowledge, to move humanity in search of greater wisdom. He wanted to spread peace and harmony in our world. In this I guess he failed. Is that true, Mum-Mum?"

"Oh, but Arthur," replied Mum-Mum, "Tut did change the world in a way. Entombed with his boyish things—his arsenal of wooden snake batons and archery equipment as well as his bows and ivory boomerangs—Tut became a boy living as a boy forever, reminding us of the innocence and beauty of childhood."

Mum-Mum continued: "Now, we don't exactly know what Bun-Bun managed with these superpowers, do we? But maybe his ultimate success or failure depends on what we do now. It's quite a challenge, Arthur, but with your gentleness and curiosity and, yes, your wonderful imagination, you can lead the way." Mum-mum kissed the top of Arthur's head and in that moment, it dawned on him that he was indeed a boy king.

Later that afternoon, when Arthur was cleaning up his room, he found a note and a pictogram in his pocket. They were from Bun-Bun:

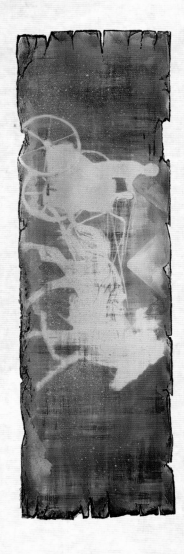

Dear Arthur,

I trust that you are reading this from the safety of your home and that dear Mum-Mum is well. Arthur, you must know: I've tried to change history and in at least one way, I'll have succeeded. The boy king will live forever . . . showing the world the purity of play he learned from you. Tut's things will have more value as art than as gold. In the end, he'll have his toys. Remember Arthur, imagination is never imaginary. It's real. The mass of starlight that evolved into human consciousness wonders not just where it came from but where it's going.

The note made Arthur dizzy with excitement, and as he sat to puzzle through it, he noticed a stuffed ear poking out of the messy clutter of his room. For a moment, his heart jumped and he thought Bun-Bun had returned, but that was impossible. It was Bunabooboo. Unlike Bun-Bun, Bunabooboo's fur was bright, new, and clean. Arthur placed the rabbit on his bed and looked at it for a time.

"Are you just gonna keep staring at me," Bunabooboo said, "or shall we have a blast changing the world?"

ACKNOWLEDGMENTS

We the authors would like to thank our friend Vijay Balakrishnan for guiding us on this journey and helping us with the editing process. We would also like to thank Elizabeth Franklin who kindly introduced us to Francis Ricciardone, the President of The American University in Cairo (AUC), who, having read the book, has been a great support. How fortunate we are to have found this home with AUC.